CONTENTS

AT A GLANCE   4

INTRODUCTION   6
THE FIRST TO KNOW

CHAPTER ONE   14
WHAT IS SOCIAL MEDIA'S IMPACT
ON THE NEWS?

CHAPTER TWO   28
WHAT IS THE HISTORY OF
SOCIAL MEDIA AND THE NEWS?

CHAPTER THREE   42
WHAT ARE EXAMPLES OF
SOCIAL MEDIA'S EFFECT ON THE NEWS?

CHAPTER FOUR   58
HOW CAN I GET RELIABLE
NEWS THROUGH SOCIAL MEDIA?

Glossary   74
Source Notes   75
For Further Research   76
Index   78
Image Credits   79
About the Author   80

AT A GLANCE

- Many people use social media platforms such as Facebook and Twitter. They get a lot of their news from these services.

- Television news networks, newspapers, and online news organizations use social media platforms to reach larger audiences.

- Social media users often share news with their friends and followers. But not all of the shared information is reliable.

- Social media can spread news fast. Sometimes news pops up on social media before professional news outlets hear about it.

- Some social media posts have live videos of events. These videos have helped bring attention to many important issues.

MEDIA LITERACY

HOW SOCIAL MEDIA IMPACTS NEWS

by Tammy Gagne

BrightPoint Press

San Diego, CA

© 2022 BrightPoint Press
an imprint of ReferencePoint Press, Inc.
Printed in the United States

For more information, contact:
BrightPoint Press
PO Box 27779
San Diego, CA 92198
www.BrightPointPress.com

ALL RIGHTS RESERVED.

No part of this work covered by the copyright hereon may be reproduced or used in any form or by any means—graphic, electronic, or mechanical, including photocopying, recording, taping, web distribution, or information storage retrieval systems—without the written permission of the publisher.

LIBRARY OF CONGRESS CATALOGING-IN-PUBLICATION DATA

Names: Gagne, Tammy, author.
Title: How social media impacts news / Tammy Gagne.
Description: San Diego, CA : BrightPoint Press, [2022]. | Series: Media literacy | Includes bibliographical references and index. | Audience: Grades 7-9
Identifiers: LCCN 2021009954 (print) | LCCN 2021009955 (eBook) | ISBN 9781678201968 (hardcover) | ISBN 9781678201975 (eBook)
Subjects: LCSH: Online journalism--United States--Juvenile literature. | Fake news--Juvenile literature. | Disinformation--United States--Juvenile literature. | Social media--Influence--Juvenile literature.
Classification: LCC PN4784.O62 G35 2022 (print) | LCC PN4784.O62 (eBook) | DDC 070.973--dc23
LC record available at https://lccn.loc.gov/2021009954
LC eBook record available at https://lccn.loc.gov/2021009955

- Social media posts may have opinions instead of facts. Some include outright lies.

- People can find reliable news on social media. They can look critically at the information. They can learn the difference between real and fake news.

INTRODUCTION

THE FIRST TO KNOW

Amelia saw her dad's car pull up in the school parking lot. She had barely buckled her seat belt when he started marveling about the latest Mars **rover** landing.

"I heard NASA got video of the rover touching down on Mars," he said. "We can watch it together as soon as we get home."

Teens might help teach their parents how to use social media.

"I've actually already seen it," Amelia told him. She felt bad as she watched her dad's excitement level drop. "But I'd love to watch it again with you," Amelia assured him. "It was really cool."

"Where did you see it?" he asked. "I heard NASA wasn't releasing the video until after 2:00 p.m." He glanced at the dashboard clock. It was only seventeen minutes past the hour.

"Mom posted a link to it on Facebook," Amelia explained. "I watched it on my phone while I was waiting for you to pick me up."

Her dad could never get to a news story faster than her or her mom. He wasn't on social media. But Amelia and her mother loved the different social media platforms. Their news feeds were constantly updating.

People can access social media accounts on platforms such as Facebook through computers or smartphones.

They could hear about many different things happening in the world.

"Was there sound too?" her dad asked.

"In a separate recording," Amelia said.

"Mom posted that too. She said the rover

caught the sound of wind. But I wasn't able to hear it with all the other students talking." She exaggerated her disappointment. Her dad knew what she was doing, but he smiled anyway. The rest of the way home, they talked excitedly about the sound the rover picked up on Mars. Amelia knew her dad was happy they could listen to the Martian sounds for the first time together.

SOCIAL MEDIA'S IMPACT ON THE NEWS

Social media is a regular part of many people's lives. They use it to connect with their friends. Users may also turn to social media for their news. It's a convenient way

Social media platforms allow people to respond to different kinds of posts.

Inaccurate information might sneak into legitimate news sources. It's up to the reader or listener to think critically about the news.

to access a lot of articles. That's because news sites post many stories on social media platforms every day. Users can also see friends' posts. Some of these posts might share news content. For people on social media, the news is often just one click away.

Not all news on social media comes from reliable sources though. Sometimes it can be difficult to tell the difference between real news and fake news. People can easily spread fake news on social media sites. This can misinform their friends or followers about an issue. Fake news on social media can have real-world consequences. But news from reliable sources can help people stay in touch with the world. Learning to tell the difference is an important media literacy skill.

CHAPTER ONE

WHAT IS SOCIAL MEDIA'S IMPACT ON THE NEWS?

The term *media* refers to any form of mass communication. Television, radio, and newspapers are part of the media. Books, magazines, movies, and music are other forms. Today, the internet is an important part of the media landscape.

Millions of people tune in to nightly news broadcasts.

Social media is a way for people to connect with each other online. It can be used to build online groups. Members can share information with each other.

With help from different social media platforms, people can read and share information around the clock.

This information can be personal. Social media can also be used to spread ideas and news found in traditional media.

THE POWER OF SOCIAL MEDIA

Social media is a powerful form of mass communication. There are many popular social media services. These include Facebook, Twitter, Instagram, and TikTok. Connecting to social media is easy. Users can log on to these services from almost anywhere. They can use web browsers on computers. Social media apps are also available. These can be downloaded onto phones, tablets, and even smart watches. Some people spend hours on social media every day.

People post many things to social media. They share photos and music. They talk about their personal lives. They also share news. Most news organizations have their own social media accounts. This is a good way for news outlets to reach a large number of people. Printed newspapers are much less popular today than they were in the past. Although television news is still popular, its audience has declined over the years. But online news is becoming more and more popular.

At first, news outlets simply used social media to direct people to news stories on websites. But now, many people do not even read the full stories. They simply read headlines or watch video clips on social media. Writer Peter Suciu explains,

Some people find it convenient to use social media to check the news.

"For many readers, instead of clicking through to the actual reporting, the social media recap seems to be good enough."[1]

Many people under the age of twenty-five like to get their news on social media.

Two-thirds of people in this age range say they turn to Instagram for news. They are also twice as likely to get news from social media than from other sources. The total number of adults turning to social media for their news is increasing. In 2020, the Pew Research Center did a report. It found that

REACHING AUDIENCES

Journalists may include their social media **handles** in stories they've written. That way, their audiences can find them on social media. People can follow their accounts on services such as Twitter. The journalists may post other stories there. It helps them reach wider audiences.

53 percent of adults in the United States either sometimes or often got their news from social media.

HOW NEWS SPREADS ACROSS SOCIAL MEDIA

Every social media platform works a bit differently. Facebook is known for connecting friends and family members. Users can also follow organizations' Facebook pages. This can include news outlets. People can share links to news articles and videos. They can also post links they find online. Users can react to posts with emojis. They can also comment on posts.

Twitter lets users post text, photos, and links. But this platform limits each post to 280 characters of text. Users create posts

SOCIAL MEDIA AS RESEARCH

In 2018, Indiana University and Syracuse University did a study. They wanted to see how journalists used social media. They found 60 percent of journalists used social media to keep in touch with their audiences. But that wasn't all. About 73 percent also said they used social media to see what other people were reporting on. More than half of them also used social media to find ideas. They used the platforms to get information for their stories.

called tweets. They can also share content from other users. These are called retweets. Twitter users often retweet content posted by popular news outlets and journalists.

Instagram users mainly post photos and videos. As with other forms of social media, Instagram users can "like" posts. They can also comment on posts. Users can interact with other people. Nic Newman is a researcher. He did a study on digital news. He found that the number of people turning to Instagram for news doubled between 2018 and 2020. "Instagram's become very popular with younger people," he said.

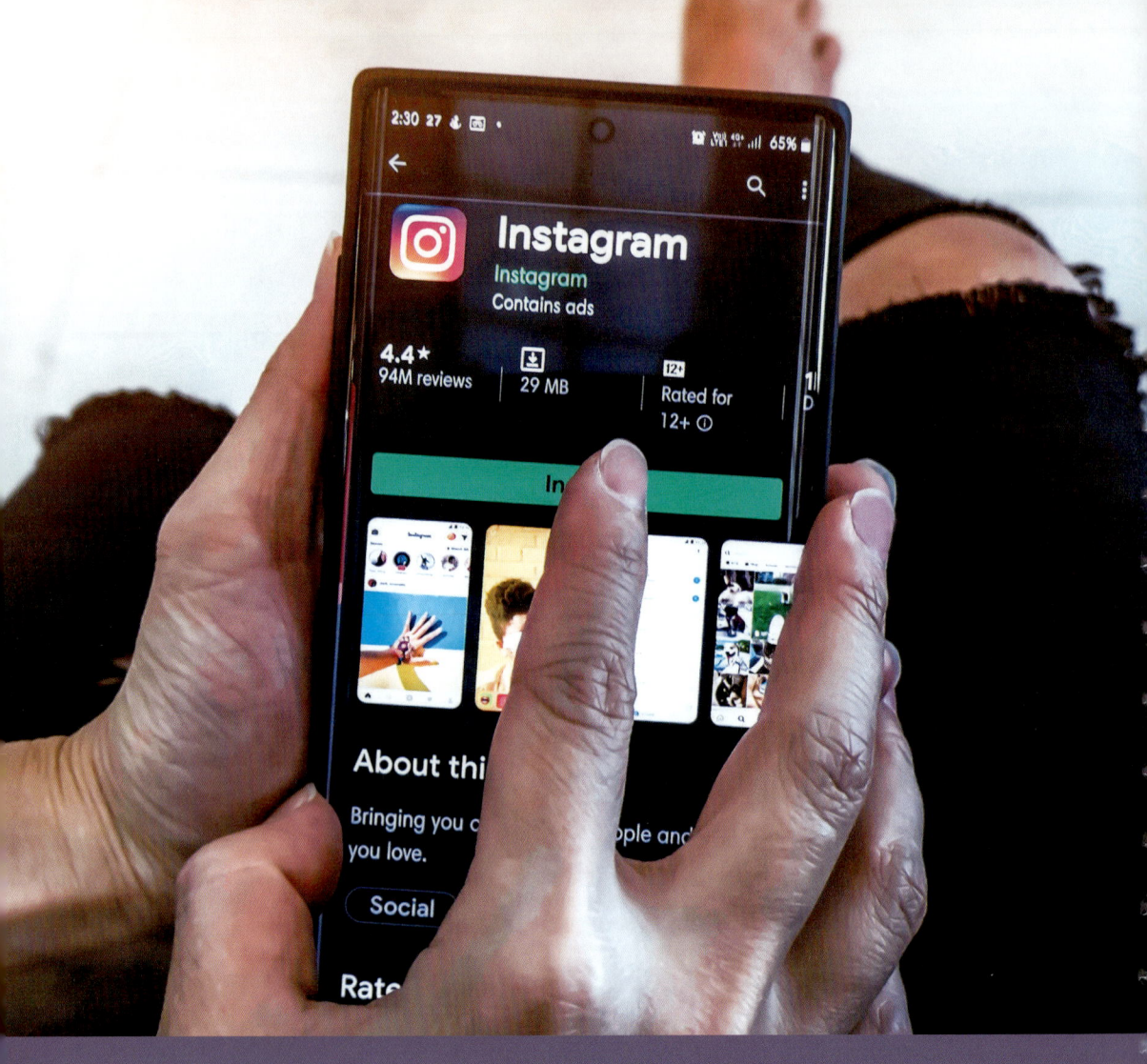

Downloading a social media app on a phone is very simple.

"They really respond well to stories that are told simply and well with visual images."[2]

There are dangers to this simplicity though.

An image and short caption cannot always tell the whole story.

WHAT SOCIAL MEDIA CAN GET WRONG

Social media is filled with blogs, videos, and other posts. Users' **biases** often influence their decisions about which content is worth their time. Filippo Menczer and Thomas Hills are professors and researchers. They know biases can affect what news people decide to listen to. According to Menczer and Hills, people who get most of their news from social media end up more biased. They're also less informed than people who turn to more reliable sources.

By using technology, people can easily share news with each other.

One of the biggest advantages of getting news from social media is how fast stories appear. But the downside is that people often spread false information this way. Journalists are trained professionals. They gather as much information as possible. They also double-check facts before publishing stories. These journalists work at good news organizations. But some stories that spread across social media are from bad sources. The information in these stories is not accurate. Social media users don't always check to make sure stories are true before sharing them. The stories may be fake, but people still believe them.

CHAPTER TWO

WHAT IS THE HISTORY OF SOCIAL MEDIA AND THE NEWS?

It may be hard to imagine a time before social media existed. But the popular platforms of today have been around only since the early 2000s. Before social media, seeking out news online took more work. Users has to log on to computers. They had

Before cell phones offered easy access to the internet, people checked their social media accounts using computers.

to visit each news website to read stories.

Today, a lot of people simply tap open their

social media accounts. They can often find

news stories posted on their feeds.

SOCIAL MEDIA EMERGES

Social media emerged in the late 1990s. It was rather simple at this time. Some early social media sites included Six Degrees and Myspace. They gave people a virtual place to meet up. People could make profiles and talk with other users.

Facebook launched in 2004, and Twitter got started in 2006. Each platform became much more popular than the social networks that came before. Most major news outlets already had websites. But now they could reach even larger audiences through social media. For news

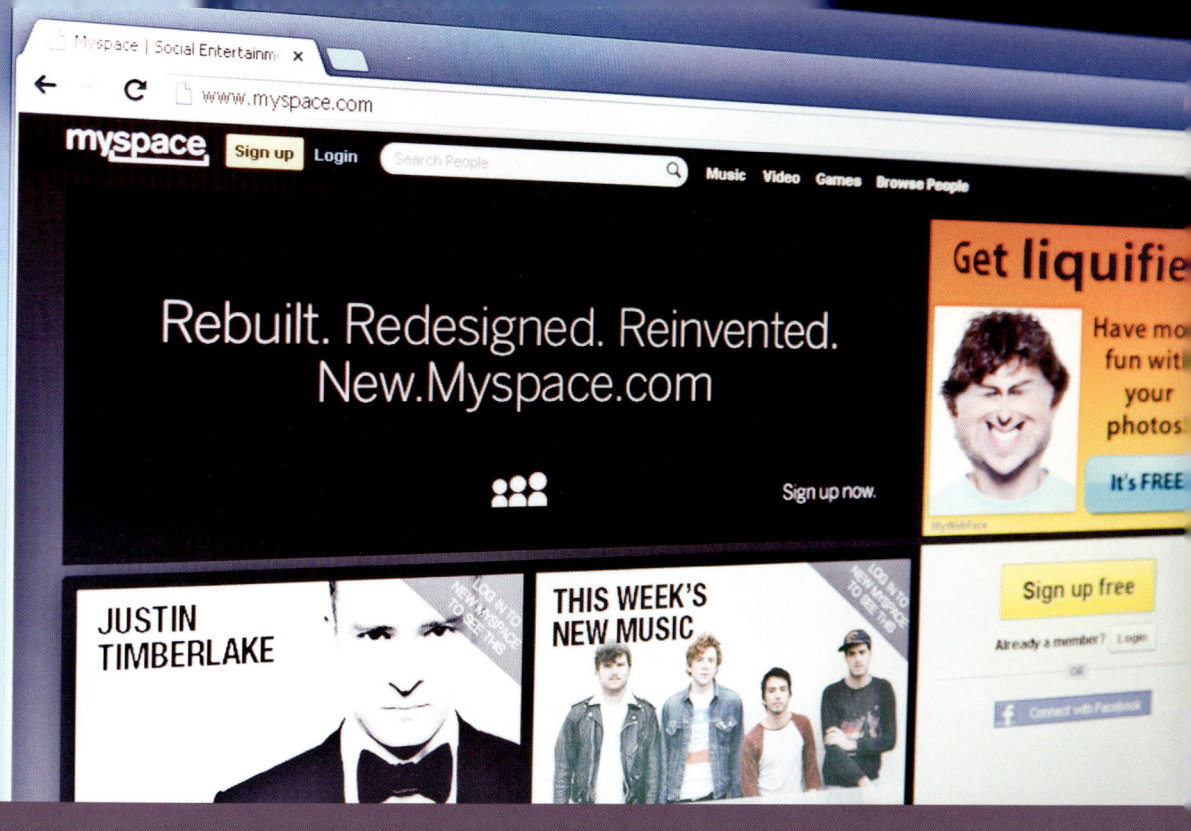

Myspace was still around in the 2020s, though it was far less popular than it had once been.

organizations, posting stories on social media was like free marketing. Social media users would share the outlets' stories for them. The news spread quickly. Soon, social media became a necessary part of journalism.

Twitter was the first social media site to group content with the hashtag (#). When people click on a hashtagged word or phrase, it shows them content other people have posted under that same tag. It helps people see what others are saying about the topic. Alexandra Samur is a journalist.

MORE TRAFFIC, LESS ATTENTION

Social media has brought more people to online news outlets. Many people learn of a news event through social media. Then they go to the news website for more information. In this way, social media has helped news outlets expand their audiences. However, the number of people who read an entire news article has gone down.

She says the hashtag has "helped political organizers and average citizens mobilize, promote, and create awareness for critical (and not so critical) social issues."[3] People began using hashtags on Twitter in 2007. But soon many other social media sites adopted this simple way to group content. It was yet another way to connect people who shared similar ideas on social media.

HEARING IT ON SOCIAL MEDIA FIRST

Before social media, people watched breaking news stories on television. But social media quickly began scooping major

Breaking news stories discuss newly available information about ongoing events.

news networks. This means it started beating other outlets to big stories.

An early example of this happened in 2009. An airplane left an airport in New York. It was headed to North Carolina. But something went wrong just after takeoff. A flock of geese flew into the plane. The birds badly damaged the plane's engines. The aircraft needed to make an emergency landing. Captain Chesley Sullenberger landed the plane on the Hudson River. He saved the lives of all 150 passengers. This was a huge news story. Soon it would be all over television. But the first reports of the event appeared on social media.

Janis Krums was riding a New York ferry when the plane landed on the water. The ferry rushed toward the downed aircraft. Krums opened his Twitter app. He posted

With the help of phones and social media, people are able to share live updates on important news.

a photo and typed, "There's a plane in the Hudson. I'm on the ferry going to pick up the people. Crazy."⁴ Krum had 170 followers. Many of them quickly shared the news with others. Soon the tweet went **viral**. It was an early example of how social media could affect the way people got their news.

PUTTING NEWS IN THE PALMS OF PEOPLE'S HANDS

Smartphones, tablets, and smart watches offered more ways for people to get on social media. They allowed people to access social media through apps. Now people didn't have to use computers to reach social media platforms. All they had to do to open an app was touch a screen.

Smart devices quickly became a big part of people's lives. In 2013, the average person spent eighty-eight minutes each

People can get a lot of different applications on their smart watches. They can even sign in to their social media accounts.

day consuming media on a mobile device. By 2019, the number had increased to 203 minutes. People wanted news fast. Will Tran is a television news reporter in San Francisco, California. He explains, "No one is going to wait around anymore for the 5 p.m. newscast to get a breaking news story that happened at noon or 1 p.m."[5] People want to be updated in real time.

NEWS VS. SOCIAL MEDIA POSTS

Journalists learn how to report the news responsibly. They gather as many facts as possible. They talk to experts and witnesses of events. People posting to their own social media accounts rarely hold themselves to these kinds of standards. Some tell only part of a story. Others post outright lies.

In 2016, a false story spread across social media. It involved a Washington, DC, pizzeria. The story said children were being harmed in the restaurant. It also claimed several Democratic politicians were involved. After reading the story, a man named Edgar Maddison Welch went to the restaurant. He was armed. He fired his gun. Welch pointed it at customers and employees. People

FAKE NEWS TRAVELS FAST

In 2018, researchers at the Massachusetts Institute of Technology did a study. They wanted to see how fast truth and lies spread across Twitter. They found that fake news spreads on Twitter faster than true stories. The difference was significant. Twitter users were 70 percent more likely to retweet a fake story than a true one. True stories took six times longer to reach a total of 1,500 people.

Some people were convinced that politicians were trafficking children at a pizzeria. This conspiracy theory was called Pizzagate.

were terrified. Welch was arrested before the situation could get further out of control. He said he was investigating the story he'd read. Welch's reaction showed the dangers of false information online.

CHAPTER THREE

WHAT ARE EXAMPLES OF SOCIAL MEDIA'S EFFECT ON THE NEWS?

False stories of voter **fraud** began to spread across social media shortly after the 2020 presidential election. President Donald Trump had lost the election to Joe Biden. However, he used

Some people who believed voter fraud happened in the 2020 election went to Stop the Steal rallies.

his social media accounts to announce that it had been stolen from him. Many of his supporters retweeted his claim. It quickly spread across social media.

LIES, LAWSUITS, AND THE FIRST AMENDMENT

Trump had no proof for his claim. But he kept posting about it. He and other Republicans also filed lawsuits to challenge the results. Judges rejected the claims that votes had been tampered with. Still, people continued to believe the fake news. A large group of Trump supporters listened to the president speak in Washington, DC, on January 6, 2021. Trump told them to fight the results. His supporters then stormed the US Capitol building. Inside, lawmakers were

Some Capitol rioters attacked police officers.

certifying the election results. Five people died in the riot.

Several social media sites banned Trump. They said he helped fuel the violence through their platforms. But many of his social media followers continued to believe and share his false claims.

Banning such a powerful person from social media sparked a national debate. Many Trump supporters said the ban violated the First Amendment. Part of this

---

BERNIE SANDERS, THE MEME

President Joe Biden's **inauguration** took place on a cold day in January 2021. Bernie Sanders is a Vermont senator. He wore practical clothes to the special event. Someone took a photo of Sanders slouched in his chair. Some people thought the photo was funny. They started making memes about Sanders. Memes are funny or interesting images that spread far and wide. Thousands of Sanders memes spread on social media.

amendment involves freedom of speech. Daphne Keller is a lawyer. She deals with internet law. She says, "The First Amendment is a constraint on the power of government. It doesn't apply to Twitter."[6] Social media sites can make their own rules. People who use the platforms accept these rules as part of their user agreements.

SPEAKING OUT AGAINST RACISM

In May 2020, a Black man named George Floyd died in police custody. An officer knelt on his neck for around nine minutes. Floyd told the officer that he could not breathe.

After George Floyd was killed, millions of people across the United States participated in peaceful protests against police violence.

But the officer didn't move. Floyd was pronounced dead a short time later.

A witness recorded the event. She posted the video to Facebook. The video quickly spread. The story became national news. Many people were outraged. It wasn't the first time white police officers had used excessive force on Black people. Many people felt this event put a spotlight on the problem of **police brutality** against people of color in the United States. Many Americans saw this as part of a pattern of unnecessary violence and racism. They wanted it to stop. They showed how they felt by **protesting**.

Social media played a significant role. First, it helped spread the video showing what happened. Afterward, people used Facebook and Twitter to spread the word about the protests. Large protests took place in cities all over the United States.

Social media helped open many people's eyes to the problem of police brutality. Shira Ovide is a journalist. She works for the *New York Times*. She explained, "Part of

---

SEEING MORE OF THE STORY

Journalists need time to reach the scene of an event as it is happening. But most people already at the scene have smartphone cameras. Smartphones have changed how some events are reported. Witnesses can post pictures and videos to social media as events happen. They can even stream live video online. This allows audiences to see more of the story.

what social media does is allow us to see a reality that has been entirely visible to some people and invisible to others. As those injustices become visible, meaningful change follows."[7] The protests dominated the news. Lawmakers responded. Some of them proposed new laws against police brutality.

SPREADING INFORMATION ABOUT COVID-19

In 2020, a disease called COVID-19 was spreading around the globe. It was caused by a virus. It made many people sick. People everywhere wanted information

Many people took precautions while in public to avoid getting and spreading COVID-19.

about this new disease. News stories told

the public how easily COVID-19 spread.

They also discussed how deadly it could

be. Many people wanted to know what they could do to protect themselves.

Health experts went on the news. They told people what they knew about COVID-19. Eventually, the experts suggested that people wear masks while in public. They also recommended that people practice social distancing. This meant staying 6 feet (1.8 m) away from others. These things would help slow the virus's spread. That, in turn, would help hospitals not get overloaded with sick patients.

Social media helped spread these public health messages. But it spread a lot of

Some people relied heavily on social media to get news about COVID-19.

misinformation about COVID-19 too. People shared stories about treatments and cures. Much of this information was false. Some of it was even dangerous.

Some social media posts claimed the virus wasn't real. Others said the media was exaggerating it to scare people. Many people believed these false news stories. Some of them chose not to wear masks. They gathered with other people. Often the number of COVID-19 cases went up after large gatherings took place. Within about a year, more than 2 million people around the world had died from COVID-19.

Even people who are aware of false information can become victims of it. Yang Cheng is a communications professor at North Carolina State University. She did

Today's technology allows people to access news quickly.

a study on COVID-19 misinformation.

She said, "People believe they are less

vulnerable toward misinformation about

COVID-19 than others. This personal bias makes it hard for people to identify misinformation or seek out media literacy training, because they think everyone needs the training more than they do."[8]

When used correctly, social media has been a good tool in the fight against COVID-19. Federal, state, and local governments used social media to provide safety tips and other medical advice. They also used social media to spread the word about vaccination timelines. These platforms even helped scientists all over the world work together to fight the pandemic.

CHAPTER FOUR

HOW CAN I GET RELIABLE NEWS THROUGH SOCIAL MEDIA?

Social media can be a useful tool. It can help people keep up with what's happening in the world. However, it can also spread misinformation. Sometimes it can even quickly spread fake news.

People can look critically at news sources found on social media. They can have conversations with others about how reliable the content is.

MISLEADING CONTENT AND FAKE NEWS

Some news stories have mistakes. In these situations, the journalists did not intend to mislead anyone. But false information was still included. A reputable news outlet will post a correction when it uncovers a mistake. This is a follow-up to the original story. It clearly states the accurate information. A mistake in a story does not mean the entire story is fake news.

    Some social media users also have blogs. Articles written by bloggers can also have inaccurate information. Most news organizations have standards for fact

Anyone can have a blog. Some authors research the topics they're discussing, but others may not.

checking. They also expect their journalists to write as objectively as possible. Bloggers do not have to follow these kinds of standards. They can say whatever they like.

Michael Lewis is a writer. He pointed out the danger of blogs and other online content. He said, "Unlike traditional news media, there are few if any regulations governing the content of blogs, social media messages, and status updates. In other words, almost anyone can publish anything on the web without concern for quality or accuracy."[9]

Fake news takes misinformation to a more dangerous level. People make these stories to intentionally mislead people. *Fake news* has become a popular term in politics. Both Democrats and Republicans have accused each other of spreading fake news stories. But sometimes people in other countries play a role too. This happened during the 2016 presidential election. After the election, American intelligence agencies did an investigation. They found that people from Russia posted many fake news stories. Their goal was to generate conflict. They wanted to influence the election's outcome. Many social media users read

INFORMATION OVERLOAD

Some people like to constantly check the news. They often do this when a big event, such as an election, happens. They may think having more information will give them more control. But that is not always the case. Some people find that checking social media for updates makes them feel more anxious.

these stories. They believed them. Then they shared the fake information. They also may have cast their votes with it in mind.

CHECK THE SOURCES

The key to getting reliable news on social media is asking the right questions. People often post links to articles. To see if the news is real, people can look at what group is reporting the story. Does the article come from a reputable news source? If people don't recognize the source, they can do some more research. They can check out the source's "About" page. This page tells readers more about the organization. It also

Taking time to research news sources can help people avoid unreliable information.

gives information about who runs it. If this page is missing or has ridiculous claims, the source may not be a real news site.

A news outlet may seem legitimate. But people should still check the story carefully. Unreliable sources often have false information alongside well-known facts. Does a particular part of the story seem off? If so, people can check to see if the information is available elsewhere. When a big story breaks, multiple outlets will report it. If people only find a single article about an event or topic, it could be because the story isn't true.

Many fake stories posted to social media use fear to reel people in. After reading a story, people can ask themselves if it made them feel afraid or angry. When social media users see a story that stirs up strong emotions, they often want to share it with others right away. Fake news creators know this. They want their stories to spread far and wide. They try to prey on people's feelings. It's important for people to make sure a story is legitimate before reposting it on social media.

SHARING FAKE NEWS

People often blame bots for spreading misinformation on social media. These are computer programs. They can "like," follow, and comment on posts. They can also post fake stories. The Massachusetts Institute of Technology did a study. It found that people are actually responsible for sharing most of the inaccurate information found on social media platforms.

Many journalists work hard to report on just the facts.

   Readers should also consider the person who shared the article. They can think about why that particular person was drawn to the story. Sam Harnett is a reporter. He did a story about news and social media. He found that many users share news on social media without even reading all of it. Harnett learned, "Sharing a post is often not about the information. It's about what the content signifies about the person who posted it. It's about trying to show that you are smart or woke or have certain values."[10]

SOCIAL MEDIA MONITORING

Journalists are supposed to keep their opinions out of their work. But bias can still be found in many stories. People are more likely to read articles that support views they already hold. And they are more likely to share those stories on social media. This happens even when the news isn't real.

Some social media sites have started to monitor posts. They want to reduce false or biased information. But some people don't like this. They think the platforms themselves are biased. On May 26, 2020, President Trump sent off a couple tweets. He said voting by mail would cause widespread voter fraud. He claimed that California was mailing ballots to people whether they were registered voters or not. Twitter responded by adding a disclaimer to these tweets. A blue exclamation point

Throughout the 2020 election, Twitter flagged some of President Donald Trump's tweets as being disputed and misleading.

appeared on each post. It had a link. The linked page clarified that California was sending ballots only to registered voters. Many Democrats praised Twitter for flagging false information. But many Republicans saw the move as a sign that Twitter was biased against their political party.

Social media plays an important role in how people get their news. Many people rely on these platforms for information. Sometimes people can see or read details about breaking news events. They may see these things even before major news outlets cover the stories. But fake news can also spread quickly on social media. Sometimes it's difficult to tell what's real. Before sharing stories, social media users should make sure the content reflects real events. Readers can ask questions about the story. They can look critically at the sources. They can check their own biases.

SOCIAL MEDIA CONTROL

| 62% | 21% | 15% |

■ Too much power
■ Around the right amount of power
■ Not enough power

Numbers do not equal 100% due to rounding.

Source: Elisa Shearer and Elizabeth Grieco, "Americans Are Wary of the Role Social Media Sites Play in Delivering the News," Pew Research Center, October 2, 2019. www.journalism.org.

In 2019, the Pew Research Center studied how Americans felt about social media. It surveyed thousands of US adults. It found that the majority of people surveyed thought social media platforms had too much power over the mix of news that users see.

This may protect people from believing false information. That way, people can actively seek out the best news possible on social media.

GLOSSARY

biases

slanted viewpoints based on people's personal opinions

fraud

wrongful deception intended for personal gain

handles

usernames that people or organizations go by on social media

inauguration

the formal admission of a politician to office

police brutality

excessive force used by police against everyday people

protesting

expressing disapproval, sometimes through a public demonstration

rover

a vehicle that explores the surface of another planet or moon

viral

related to an image or information that spreads quickly across the internet

SOURCE NOTES

CHAPTER ONE: WHAT IS SOCIAL MEDIA'S IMPACT ON THE NEWS?

1. Peter Suciu, "More Americans Are Getting Their News from Social Media," *Forbes*, October 11, 2019. www.forbes.com.

2. Quoted in "Instagram 'Will Overtake Twitter As a News Source,'" *BBC*, June 16, 2020. www.bbc.com.

CHAPTER TWO: WHAT IS THE HISTORY OF SOCIAL MEDIA AND THE NEWS?

3. Alexandra Samur, "The History of Social Media: 29+ Key Moments," *Hootsuite*, November 22, 2018. https://blog.hootsuite.com.

4. Quoted in Christina Zdanowicz, "'Miracle on the Hudson' Twitpic Changed His Life," *CNN*, January 15, 2014. www.cnn.com.

5. Quoted in John Boitnott, "Tech Is Changing the Way We Get Our News, and It's Not Stopping," *Inc.*, July 22, 2015. www.inc.com.

CHAPTER THREE: WHAT ARE EXAMPLES OF SOCIAL MEDIA'S EFFECT ON THE NEWS?

6. Quoted in Tyler Sonnemaker, "Twitter and Facebook Both Banned Trump from Their Platforms," *Business Insider*, January 9, 2021. www.businessinsider.com.

7. Shira Ovide, "How Social Media Has Changed Civil Rights Protests," *New York Times*, December 17, 2020. www.nytimes.com.

8. Quoted in Dennis Thompson, "Why COVID Lies on Social Media Are So Seductive," *US News*, December 14, 2020. www.usnews.com.

CHAPTER FOUR: HOW CAN I GET RELIABLE NEWS THROUGH SOCIAL MEDIA?

9. Michael Lewis, "Fake News? 8 Ways to Determine If a News Story Is Reliable," *Money Crashers*, July 3, 2018. www.moneycrashers.com.

10. Sam Harnett, "People Don't Read Everything They Share Online," *KQED*, May 17, 2018. www.kqed.org.

FOR FURTHER RESEARCH

BOOKS

Robin Terry Brown, *Breaking the News*. Washington, DC: National Geographic Kids, 2020.

Marcia S. Gresko, *How Should Extremist Content Be Regulated on Social Media?* San Diego, CA: ReferencePoint, 2021.

R. L. Van, *Identifying Fake News*. San Diego, CA: BrightPoint, 2022.

INTERNET SOURCES

Monica Anderson and Jingjing Jiang, "Teens, Social Media & Technology 2018," *Pew Research Center*, May 31, 2018. www.pewresearch.org.

Kay Boatner, "Spotting Fake News," *National Geographic Kids*, n.d. https://kids.nationalgeographic.com.

"Tips for Students on How to Identify Fake News," *University of North Dakota*, n.d. https://onlinedegrees.und.edu.

WEBSITES

Crash Course: Media Literacy
https://thecrashcourse.com/courses/medialiteracy

The Crash Course website has an informative section to help visitors develop media literacy skills. It offers many videos to teach people about this topic.

PBS: News and Media Literacy
https://tpt.pbslearningmedia.org/collection/newsandmedialiteracy

PBS's News and Media Literacy section offers articles, videos, and more to help people develop important media literacy skills.

Teaching Kids News
https://teachingkidsnews.com/fakenews

Teaching Kids News has a wide variety of articles about real-world events. Each article, no matter how complex the topic, is written in a way for students to understand.

INDEX

apps, 17, 35, 37

banned, 45–46
bias, 25, 57, 69–72
Biden, Joe, 42, 46
blogs, 25, 60–62

corrections, 60
COVID-19, 51–57

disclaimers, 70

elections, 42, 45, 63
experts, 39, 53

Facebook, 8, 17, 21, 30, 48–49
fake news, 13, 27, 39–41, 44, 55, 58, 60, 62–64, 66–67, 72
Floyd, George, 47–48
fraud, 42, 70

Harnett, Sam, 68–69
hashtags, 32–33
Hills, Thomas, 25

Indiana University, 22
Instagram, 17, 20, 23

lawsuits, 44
Lewis, Michael, 61–62

marketing, 31
memes, 46
Menczer, Filippo, 25

NASA, 6, 8
Newman, Nic, 23
newspapers, 14, 18

Ovide, Shira, 50

Pew Research Center, 20, 73
protest, 49–51

riot, 45

Samur, Alexandra, 32–33
Sanders, Bernie, 46
smart watches, 17, 37
Suciu, Peter, 18
Sullenberger, Chesley, 35
Syracuse University, 22

tablets, 17, 37
TikTok, 17
Trump, Donald, 42–46, 70
Twitter, 17, 20, 22–23, 30, 32–33, 35, 40, 47, 49, 70–71

viral, 36

witnesses, 39, 48, 50

IMAGE CREDITS

Cover: © leungchopan/Shutterstock Images
5: © Poike/iStockphoto
7: © Chaay_Tee/Shutterstock Images
9: © PK Studio/Shutterstock Images
11: © sitthiphong/Shutterstock Images
12: © Antonio Guillem/Shutterstock Images
15: © Lutsenko_Oleksandr/Shutterstock Images
16: © Vasin Lee/Shutterstock Images
19: © insta_photos/Shutterstock Images
24: © Nok Lek/Shutterstock Images
26: © filadendron/iStockphoto
29: © Denis Tabler/Shutterstock Images
31: © Tom K Photo/Shutterstock Images
34: © Tashi-Delek/iStockphoto
36: © Luna Vandoorne/Shutterstock Images
38: © Twin Design/Shutterstock Images
41: © Phil Pasquini/Shutterstock Images
43: © Brandi Lyon Photography/Shutterstock Images
45: © lev radin/Shutterstock Images
48: © Hayk_Shalunts/Shutterstock Images
52: © eldar nurkovic/Shutterstock Images
54: © Andrej Hicil/Shutterstock Images
56: © khunnok studio/Shutterstock Images
59: © Antonio Guillem/Shutterstock Images
61: © fizkes/Shutterstock Images
65: © Syda Productions/Shutterstock Images
68: © 2p2play/Shutterstock Images
71: © Ascannio/Shutterstock Images
73: © Red Line Editorial

ABOUT THE AUTHOR

Tammy Gagne has written hundreds of books for both adults and children. Some of her recent books have been about gaming disorder and anxiety. She lives in northern New England with her husband, son, and several pets.